Dear Parent: anythink

Your child's love of reading starts here!

Every child learns to read in a different way and at his or her own speed. Some go back and forth between reading levels and read favorite books again and again. Others read through each level in order. You can help your young read~ ~mprove and become more confident by encouraging h~ ~ interests and abilities. From books your child ~ ~t books he or she reads alone, there ~ y stage of reading:

SHA~

My First

Basic la~ ~ repetition, and whimsical illustrations, ideal for ~naring with your emergent reader

BEGINNING READING

Short sentences, familiar words, and simple concepts for children eager to read on their own

READING WITH HELP

Engaging stories, longer sentences, and language play for developing readers

READING ALONE

Complex plots, challenging vocabulary, and high-interest topics for the independent reader

I Can Read Books have introduced children to the joy of reading since 1957. Featuring award-winning authors and illustrators and a fabulous cast of beloved characters, I Can Read Books set the standard for beginning readers.

A lifetime of discovery begins with the magical words "I Can Read!"

Visit www.icanread.com for information
on enriching your child's reading experience.

44 Cats™

CATS ROCK!

Meatball Lampo Milady Pilou

Written by Steve Foxe

HARPER

An Imprint of HarperCollinsPublishers

Meet Lampo!

He is a natural leader

and plays the guitar.

This is one talented cat.

He's also a lead singer!

Milady plays music with Lampo.

She plays the bass guitar.

The bass keeps the rhythm

and makes the tunes funky!

Milady's bass is pink!

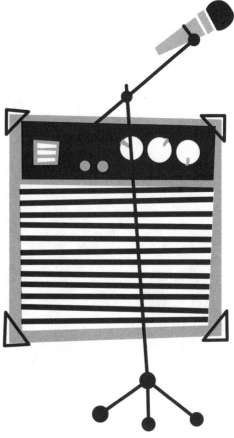

Everyone loves Pilou's big eyes
and cute smile.

But don't let them fool you!

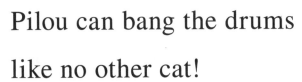

Pilou can bang the drums
like no other cat!

And then there's Meatball.

He is one funny cat.

The band members always laugh

when Meatball is around.

10

Not only is he funny,

but he can rock out on the piano!

Together, Lampo, Milady,
Pilou, and Meatball are the Buffycats!
The Buffycats love to rock out.
Rocking out means
playing music together.

Through the power of music
and friendship, they make super tunes.
No, really.
Their music is super powered!

With Granny Pina's help,

the cats make super powered music.

Granny Pina takes care of the cats.

She makes sure they are happy

and well fed!

She's a great cook.

Her specialty is

super powered noodles.

Granny Pina makes her special noodles.

When the cats eat the noodles,

they sing the special noodles song.

The yummy noodles
give them super energy!

The noodles have sauce and meatballs.

Lampo and Milady eat the noodles.

It's a big bowl!

They now have super energy.

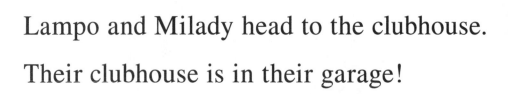

Lampo and Milady head to the clubhouse.

Their clubhouse is in their garage!

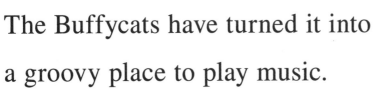

The Buffycats have turned it into

a groovy place to play music.

All cats are welcome at the clubhouse!

Lampo and Milady start to rock out.

Lampo plays guitar,

and Milady plays her bass.

They sing together.

The two friends
are in perfect harmony.
Their music is powerful!

Some cats aren't friendly.

Boss doesn't like the Buffycats.

He wants to ruin their fun.

Blister and Scab are his sidekicks.

Don't get on their bad side!

Then there's Winston.

Boss lives with Winston.

They live next door to the Buffycats.

Winston also wants to ruin

the Buffycats' fun.

Winston wants to tear down their clubhouse.

Buffycats stand up to bullies. Together, they use their powers for good.

Not only do noodles
give them super powers,
but friendship does too!

The Buffycats help every cat
in the neighborhood.
They inspire them all
to stand up to bullies.
But sometimes not just cats
need their help.

The Buffycats help those in need.

Even dogs!

So rock out with these friends.

You can be a Buffycat too!